Lady Kaguya's Secret

adapted from an
ancient Japanese tale

Art by Jirina Marton

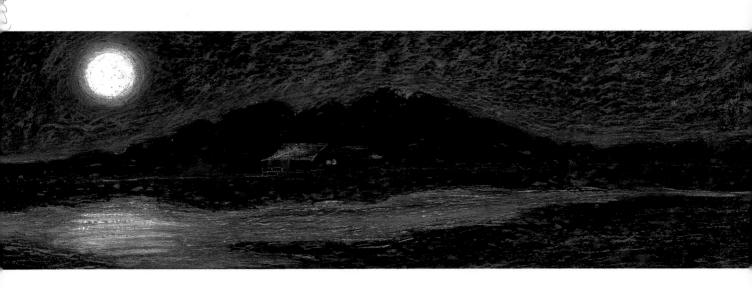

Annick Press • Toronto • New York

Long ago at the foot of Mount Fuji there lived Taketori, the old bamboocutter, and his wife.

Early each morning Taketori set out to cut bamboo in a nearby forest. One day, as he approached a familiar grove, a soft glow emanated from one of the trees. He cut it down and could hardly believe his eyes. Before him, right on the trunk, lay a tiny baby girl. Her beauty radiated like the most exquisite flower and lit up the forest.

Gently, his heart pounding, the old man carried the tiny girl back to his cottage.

"Look at what I found today!" he called out to his wife. Flushed with joy she picked up the baby. And as no one came to claim her, they named her Kaguya-hime, "Radiant Princess," and they became a happy family.

The childless couple had been poor, but from that day on, whenever Taketori returned to the bamboo grove, he found nuggets of pure gold in the trunks he cut. This good fortune enabled the couple to surround the girl with exquisite things and the finest teachers. Very quickly she grew into a beautiful and bright young maiden.

News of her mysterious ways and extraordinary beauty had travelled far and wide, and young noblemen arrived from all over the land just to catch a glimpse of her. Alas, the Lady Kaguya did not take any notice of them, and when winter came, just five ardent admirers remained, hoping to conquer Kaguya's heart.

One day Taketori spoke to his daughter: "Kaguya, you are a fine and mature young girl with many skills, almost grown up. While your mother and I would be very sad to see you part from us, it is customary for a young woman to choose a husband." But Kaguya replied, "My honourable father, I am eager to please you and my mother in all ways, but I must tell you that I will not marry."

Kaguya was well aware of her parents' deep disappointment, and she finally spoke: "I do not wish to insult anyone. If it means bringing honour to the family, then I will agree to meet the suitors waiting outside. I will send each on a quest to see who is the most courageous." These words pleased the parents very much, and the father went to make the announcement.

The first suitor, a Prince, stepped proudly into the cottage and bowed. Overwhelmed by Kaguya's beauty, he fell in love at once.

"I have come to propose," he said.

"I am only a bamboocutter's daughter," began the Lady Kaguya.

"No matter," he replied. "And I am willing to do anything to prove my devotion. Name the task."

"Very well, then," said the Lady Kaguya, "I should like to see the stone bowl of the Buddha."

Though stunned at this request, the Prince returned to his palace and prepared to set sail for India. When he learned just how arduous the journey was, he changed his mind and was not heard from again.

The next Prince to ask for Kaguya's hand in marriage was one of the wealthiest men in Japan. When he beheld Kaguya's beauty, he promised her a golden palace.

"I seek something still more precious," she replied. "Bring me a golden bow from the sacred tree of Mount Horai."

"You shall have it, my lady," promised the Prince, and he departed.

No one heard from him for three long years. Then one morning a maid brought the Lady Kaguya a most exquisite-looking box. What if this suitor had truly succeeded in fulfilling the quest?

But soon her parents heard a little laugh on the verandah. It was a fine work of jewellery Kaguya beheld, six emeralds set in leaves of gold, but a man-made branch, she was certain. In silence, Lady Kaguya returned the box to the waiting Prince. Aware that his deception had been discovered, he bowed and left, never to return.

The third suitor was a Chief Counsellor of the district, and a highly respected man. Otomo No Miyuki was thought to be the most courageous man in the land. Kaguya looked serious as she spoke.

"The task for you is hard and extremely dangerous. You may not wish to take it on."

"What could it be that I should refuse?" asked Otomo. "No sacrifice shall be too great to win your hand in marriage."

"Very well, then," said the Lady Kaguya. "In a deep cave in a land across the sea there lives a fierce dragon that destroys anyone who attempts to go ashore. His forehead is adorned with a magnificent jewel. Bring me this gem."

Determined to win the lovely lady's hand, Otomo gathered his most loyal servants, who made ready a boat, and they sailed away. But on the twelfth day at sea a typhoon struck. Lightning bolted out of a black sky and mountainous waves threatened to capsize the small vessel.

The servants turned to their master. "We are nearing the land of the dragon, Sire," they wailed, "it will not allow us to approach the shore. Let us turn around or we shall perish!"

Otomo looked at his men in anguish. He fell to his knees and asked the dragon for forgiveness, then steered the boat away to a small island, where they remained for many days and nights, the master too ill to travel.

When news of the five noblemen's failure reached the Emperor, he was curious. Who was this extraordinary young woman whose beauty inspired some of the finest men in the land to attempt such deeds? He sent a messenger to the bamboocutter's house, inviting them to visit with their daughter. But the Lady Kaguya refused to appear at court.

Irritated, the
Emperor rode his
horse to their home to
punish them, but when
the Lady Kaguya was
summoned and he saw
this most exquisite young
woman, his anger
disappeared and he
fell in love at once.

A proud and powerful man, he announced to the bamboocutter, "I am the Emperor. Your daughter will become my wife."

Lady Kaguya spoke at last. "Forgive me, dear parents, for my long silence. The time has come that I disclose a secret. I must not marry any human being on earth. I am not a creature of this world, but a lady of the moon. One day I shall have to return."

The parents stood side by side, unable to believe what they had just heard.

Deeply disappointed and saddened, the Emperor rode back to his palace. Still, he could not put the Lady Kaguya out of his mind.

Messengers began to arrive at the bamboocutter's house, bearing presents: a bowl of exotic fruit, a bouquet of the most fragrant flowers, a sparkling gem, and finally poems, written by the Emperor only for her. So fine were these poems, so noble in spirit, that in time she began to respond. Silver-speckled small scrolls would arrive at the palace, bringing the Emperor a happiness he had never known.

Meanwhile, Taketori and his wife had become deeply concerned about their beloved daughter, for they had found her unhappy and grieving lately, standing at the window late at night, wiping away tears.

"What is it, Kaguya, that gives you so much pain?" they inquired.

"My father, my mother," Kaguya replied, "for many nights I have pleaded with the Moon King to let me stay here on earth, but to no avail. At midnight he will come to take me back."

The mother and father were stricken with grief. Word was sent at once to the Emperor, who arrived immediately with his palace guard to protect the Lady Kaguya. They were stationed all around the grounds, bows and arrows at the ready. Kaguya was held tight by her mother. Out on the verandah stood her father, his axe in hand, determined to protect her. The Emperor was by his side.

"No one will defeat the Emperor's guard," murmured the mother.

"But the moon warriors are immortal," sighed Kaguya with tears in her eyes.

At the stroke of midnight a silvery cloud lifted from the surface of the full moon and approached the earth. It hovered just above Taketori's house. The father stood frozen as his axe clattered to the ground. The Emperor too was struck immobile by an invisible force. The palace guards stood like objects of stone.

From the centre of the fierce light a powerful voice was heard: "I have come for my daughter."

Taketori roused himself and called out, "But she has been our daughter all these years. She is now one of us!"

"Daughter," called the voice, "come forth."

Shivering, the Lady Kaguya stepped forward.

"My Lord," she pleaded, "I weep for I wish to stay."

"Foolish words, my daughter. Would you live and suffer and die like these mortals?"

"Yes, indeed. Let me stay, I beseech you one last time."

In answer a shining goblet appeared in front of Kaguya. It contained the elixir of eternal life.

"Drink from this cup," commanded the voice.

Kaguya hesitated, turning to the motionless Emperor. Then she obeyed. Right away her body took on an ethereal appearance as though lit from within.

"Now this," continued the voice from the cloud, and a sparkling robe appeared. The light was blinding. Everyone held their breath.

"Give me a moment longer," Kaguya whispered. "Once I shall wear this robe, I will forget all earthly joys and sorrows, and will never remember any of you again."

She knelt before her parents. "Drink from this cup," she pleaded. "I shall not be here to comfort you when your time comes to die. I would prefer you lived forever."

But the parents shook their heads. "If you go, why should we wish to live? You have brought us nothing but joy. Now we would rather pass on."

At this, Kaguya rushed into her room. Pouring the elixir of life into a crystal bottle, she wrote one last note to the Emperor, ending in these words:

My Dearest Friend,
It is true that I could never share your life.
Yet you have brought me such happiness.
Let me bestow on you the gift of immortality.
My last memory will be of you.

She returned, passing bottle and scroll into the Emperor's hands.

She embraced her
parents, took the cloak
around her shoulders and
was gone in the icy light of
the silver cloud, which
instantly disappeared with
her into the night sky.

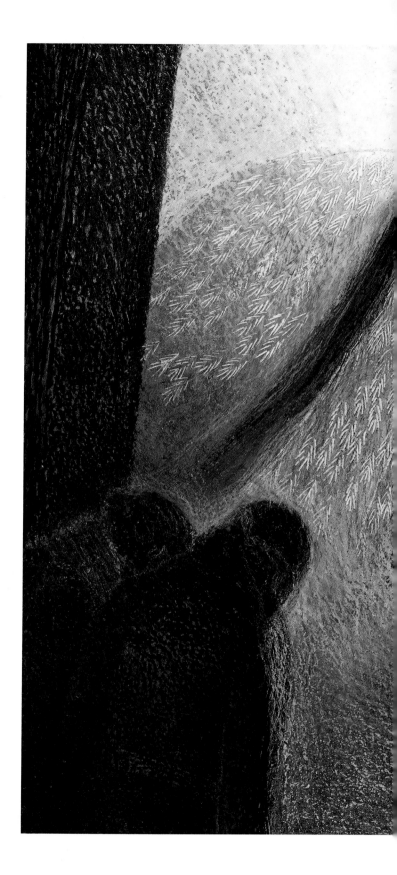

Grief-stricken, the Emperor read her words. He too refused her gift of immortality. Instead, he embarked on a journey to the mountain top closest to the moon. There, he set fire to the scroll and poured the elixir over the flames, calling out:

"Oh, may the smoke reach her and may she remember for just an instant!"

And from that day a small trace of smoke was seen drifting towards the sky from the top of Mount Fuji.

The artist wishes to express her thanks to
Kazuko Sekine, Yumiko Fukumoto and
especially to Toshi Aoyagi

The editor gratefully acknowledges the
expert advice of Kenneth L. Richard and
Naomi Wakan

Annick Press gratefully acknowledges the support of the Canada Council and the Japan Foundation.

Cataloguing in Publication Data
Lady Kaguya's secret : a Japanese folktale
ISBN 1-55037-441-9
1. Tales - Japan. I. Marton, Jirina.
PZ8.1.L33 1997 j398.20952 C97-930351-6

The art in this book was rendered in oil pastels.
The text was typeset in President.

Distributed in Canada by:
Firefly Books Ltd.
3680 Victoria Park Avenue
Willowdale, ON M2H 3K1

Published in the U.S.A. by Annick Press (U.S.) Ltd.
Distributed in the U.S.A. by:
Firefly Books (U.S.) Inc.
P.O. Box 1338, Ellicott Station
Buffalo, NY 14205

Printed in Hong Kong.